Camdean School

KU-067-990

THE CORMORANT

Written by
Susan Griffiths

Illustrated by
Rae Dale

PROPERTY OF

29 MAR 2004

CAMDEAN PRIMARY

HORWITZ
MARTIN
EDUCATION

Contents

Chapter 1

A Grand Day For Fishing

For as long as anyone could remember, Fairtide had been a prosperous fishing village. The warm, blue sea that lapped up against the shore was the main reason why the inhabitants of Fairtide made a good living.

Each morning, before the golden sun rose over the eastern horizon, a colourful fleet of small fishing boats set off from the Fairtide Pier. If the wind was blowing in the right direction, jolly sea shanties could be heard floating back across the dark, moonlit water as the fishing boats headed for the ocean.

It's off to sea we go, my hearties,
It's off to sea we go!

And when the nets are cast, my hearties,
Yes, when the nets are cast,

We'll watch the sun rise-o, my hearties,
We'll watch the sun rise-o!

Each afternoon, beneath clouds of hungry seagulls, the colourful wooden fishing boats would return laden with silvery mackerel, sleek trevally and heavy grey cod. The freshly caught fish would be packed into boxes of crushed ice and taken to the busy fish markets.

The very next morning they would be sold to eager fishmongers for shops and restaurants. Fairtide had a reputation for supplying the freshest, finest fish throughout the whole country.

Amongst the boats that fished the plentiful seas off
Fairtide was a cheerful fishing vessel named the
Cormorant. Her captain, Oliver Grout, was over
seventy years old. He had been sailing in and out
of Fairtide for almost sixty of those years.

Oliver Grout knew everything there was to know
about the sea and fishing. For the past year,
his grandson, Sam, had been working on the
Cormorant, to watch and learn from the
experienced sea captain.

One frosty morning, well before the first rays of the rising sun appeared over the horizon, Oliver and Sam walked down to Fairtide Pier. Their breath hung like clouds of steam as their footsteps echoed around the cobbled street.

"Aye, lad, it looks like a grand day for fishing," Oliver observed, as he peered towards the stars twinkling in the sky. "Clear and bright. We'll head towards the reef this morning. There'll be good fishing around the reef today."

"Will you teach me some more knots later?" asked Sam. Knots were very important for fishermen, who had to tie and untie ropes and lines and cords quickly on their boats.

"Aye, lad, after we put the nets down. I'll show you the 'half-blood knot' and the 'sailor's noose'."

Sam grinned. He liked the names of those knots. He loved going fishing with his grandfather, and was already dreaming of the day when he would be captain of his own little fishing boat.

On board the *Cormorant*, Oliver and Sam checked their nets, ropes, engines and safety gear. Around them, through the darkness, the other fishermen slowly arrived on the wharf, calling out cheery greetings to each other.

Soon, the fleet was ready to head off towards the east.

"What shanty shall we sing this morning?" asked Sam. Oliver pushed his faded captain's hat back, and scratched his head.

"I know," he said. "I'll teach you the one about the mermaid and the seahorse." He smiled and hummed the tune. Then he stopped.

"No, maybe I had better not. I've just remembered it's got some rude words in it. I'll think of another one."

As the *Cormorant* headed out towards the east, Oliver's voice could be heard floating back across the pier.

Slap the waves, slop the waves,
The rhythm of the sea,

The gentle beat of the sea, my hearties,
Is the only beat for me.

Far in the distance, a golden glow slowly appeared over the edge of the sea. Half an hour later, just as the piercing rays of sunlight had crept over the horizon, the *Cormorant* reached the reef. Exactly as Oliver had predicted, the day dawned clear and bright.

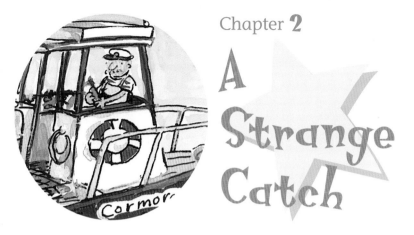

Chapter 2

A Strange Catch

"*D*rop the net over the edge, lad!" ordered Oliver. He happily stood at the wheel. Just in front of the *Cormorant*, a flock of birds circled and dived into the water. He pointed, and Sam looked up from where he was carefully arranging the *Cormorant*'s long silky net.

"That means little fish are just under the water," said Oliver. "And where there's little fish, there's big fish underneath."

With a splash, Sam tossed the floating orange
buoy that marked one end of the net into the sea.
Metre by metre, the net slithered and snaked as it
uncoiled, slowly sinking beneath the surface of the
water. Oliver turned the wheel of the *Cormorant*
and gradually circled the birds.

Suddenly, the sea started to boil.

"Look!" cried Sam, pointing towards the foaming
white water. A school of silvery mackerel had burst
to the surface and were wildly thrashing around.
Oliver almost whistled, before remembering that
whistling on board a boat was very bad luck.

"There must be some really big fish below," Oliver called out. "They're chasing the mackerel to the surface!" The birds dived speedily into the welcome feast, reappearing after a few seconds with shimmering, wriggling fishes in their beaks.

Oliver turned the *Cormorant* around in a wide circle, and slowly headed towards the buoy that marked the first end of the net. Slowly but surely, the net formed a circle around where the fish were. But just as suddenly as the action started, the splashing of the mackerel on the surface stopped.

"The mackerel are getting away," yelled Sam.

"Don't worry about them," replied his grandfather. "It's the big fish below we want. Get the boathook, lad, and pull in the first buoy."

Sam clambered over to where the long boathook lay and swung it out over the waves. Gradually, Oliver edged the *Cormorant* close enough for Sam to snare the buoy with the large hook. Quickly, he dragged it on board.

"Hitch it to the winch," ordered Oliver. Sam carefully untied the buoy from the rope attached to the net, and tied the rope to the winch. Oliver pulled a lever and metre by metre, the winch hauled the long net on board.

Sam waited quietly for the first fish to appear. Then, beneath the waves, he saw a grey shape heading towards the surface. Something was trapped in the net. Finally, it burst through the surface of the water, shiny and dripping.

"What on earth?" said Oliver, staring at the grey object.

His hands protected by strong leather gloves, Sam grasped the thing and pulled it free from the slow-moving net. He held it up, with an astonished look on his face. It was a large cod — or, to be exact, the head of a large cod. The body of the fish behind the gills was missing — cleanly sliced off as if someone had cut it off with a sharp knife. Sam dropped the head onto the deck as he spotted something else emerging from the deep sea.

In amazement, Sam saw another fish head being slowly hauled out of the sea. He turned to stare at his grandfather, who looked unsure about what to say next. In all his years of fishing in the seas off Fairtide, Oliver had never seen anything like this. An anxious look crossed his face. He had heard of this happening in a few villages far to the south — but never around Fairtide.

They worked in silence as Sam cleared fish head after fish head from the net. Not a single whole fish was caught, only the heads.

As the last of the net was hauled on board, Oliver pushed his captain's hat back and rubbed his forehead. He was worried. If this was what he thought it was, it was bad news for the people of Fairtide. Very bad news.

Sam finished tidying up the deck, and climbed up to where his grandfather was standing.

"What's going on, Grandad?" he asked, pointing back at the basket of fish heads. It was the only result of their morning's work. "We can't sell those to the market."

Oliver shook his head and gazed out across the sea. The birds had disappeared, their stomachs full and heavy with their morning feed of mackerel. The gentle slap of the waves against the sides of the *Cormorant* was the only sound.

"I've never heard of one this close to Fairtide," said Oliver, with a worried look.

"One what?" asked Sam.

Oliver took a deep breath and nodded towards the basket of fish heads.

"There's only one thing that will do that to a school of fish," he said heavily. "A *shark*."

Chapter 3

A Smelly Plan!

That afternoon back at the wharf, the news was not good. Every boat had had its catch stolen or its nets torn. For the first time in as long as anyone could remember, there would be no fresh Fairtide fish for sale at the morning market. All along the Fairtide Pier, small groups of fishermen huddled together, swapping stories about the monster from the deep.

"I saw it!" claimed one fisherman, stretching his arms as wide as he could. "It had jaws this big!"

"It looked like a submarine passing underneath us," added another. "A long grey shadow, as long as our boat!"

"It tore a hole in my net big enough for a car to drive through," said a captain. He held up the remains of a torn net and, true to his word, there was a gigantic hole ripped right through the middle.

Everyone on the Fairtide Pier was worried about what the shark would do to their livelihoods. Without fresh fish to fill up their iceboxes and sell to the markets, they would soon run out of money.

Then, Oliver said something that surprised everyone.

"Does anyone have any fish heads for sale?" he asked. "I'll buy the whole lot."

Everyone looked puzzled. No-one had anything *but* fish heads.

"What do you want fish heads for?" they asked.

"Never you mind, my hearties," grinned Oliver. "I'm buying, if you're selling."

Within minutes, Oliver had bought enough fish heads to fill a big old wooden barrel.

"What are you doing?" whispered Sam, who was also very confused.

"Don't worry, lad," grinned Oliver to his grandson. "Just give me a hand." Together, they rolled the barrel of fish heads up the cobbled street towards their house. "The others will sit there all afternoon talking — but I have a plan!"

Sam smiled back. He knew that if anything could be done about the shark, the oldest, most experienced fisherman in Fairtide would be the person to do it. When they reached their house, Oliver spent the rest of the afternoon rummaging about in the attic. Finally, Sam heard a cry of satisfaction from up in the roof.

"A-ha! I knew I had one of these somewhere."

Oliver climbed back down the ladder from the attic, clutching the most enormous fish hook Sam had ever seen. It was as long as a coat-hanger and made of hard, round steel, as thick as a broom handle.

"That fish hook looks incredible! Are we going to catch the shark with it?" asked Sam incredulously.

"Aye, lad," replied Oliver, his eyes twinkling. "We'll not only solve the problem, we'll end up sending the biggest fish ever seen to the markets." He rubbed his hands together. "We'll make more money in one day than we do in a week."

Sam reminded his grandfather about what the other fishermen had said about the shark. If they were right, the shark was a monster. How on earth would they haul a shark as big as their boat onto the deck? What would happen if it thrashed around, with snapping jaws as wide as a man's arms? And, not least of all, where would they find an icebox big enough to send an entire monster shark to market?

But Oliver was not to be put off from continuing with his plan. If there was a monster shark terrorising life in the waters off Fairtide, he would be the one to catch it.

"Now, lad, we have work to do. Let's go to the kitchen!"

For the whole of that evening, a strange, fishy smell drifted down the cobbled street and swirled around Fairtide like a bad-smelling mist.

The next morning, an hour before sunrise, Oliver and Sam were already on their boat. They had spent the evening boiling and mashing most of the fish heads into a mealy, mashed-up sort of fish soup, and refilled the barrel with the stinking mixture.

No-one else was on the pier. The other fishermen,
thinking that all they were likely to catch were
more fish heads, decided to have a sleep-in.
On his grandfather's orders, Sam untied the
Cormorant from the jetty. The night air echoed
with the gentle thud-thud of the *Cormorant*'s
engine, as she slowly headed out to sea.

The *Cormorant* reached the reef before the first rays of the sun appeared over the horizon.

"Now, we'll wait, lad," said Oliver. "As soon as the sun starts to rise, we'll swing into action."

The gentle bobbing of the *Cormorant* was peaceful and relaxing. Both Sam and Oliver sat back and quietly hummed another tune, waiting for the first light to break over the edge of the sea. Little did they know it would be the last peaceful moment in a long day to come — a day of adventure and drama.

Chapter 4

A Tug Of War

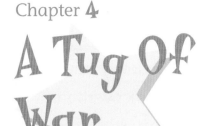

The sun was creeping skyward. "Over she goes, lad," ordered Oliver, as the sky turned from inky black to a pale bronze colour.

Both Oliver and Sam struggled to lift up the barrel and pour its contents over the side of the *Cormorant*. The smelly soup gurgled and slopped into the sea and a fishy, stinking brown stain spread out behind the little fishing boat.

"The smell of that stuff would attract a shark from ten kilometres away," said Oliver proudly. He raced back to the cabin, and carefully threaded four big fish heads that he had saved onto the massive fish hook.

Skillfully, Oliver attached the hook to the strong line wound around the winch. Using the winch lever, he slowly unwound the line and tossed the baited hook overboard. It sank beneath the water, taking fifty metres of line with it.

"Now, we wait, lad," he said. But they didn't have to wait long.

Sam watched in awe as the line, straight and taut, suddenly hissed its way out of the water. Like an arrow, it pointed to a spot about fifty metres to the east. And then the entire *Cormorant* lurched, as if it had struck a rock and been tossed back into the surf.

For a moment, even Oliver looked alarmed. He grabbed onto the railing to keep steady and yelled out, "Hold on tight, Sam!"

The line moved through the water at an amazing speed. First it pointed to the east, yet seconds later, it had swung around behind them. Then, it moved down and down.

"It's coming to get us," yelled Sam. The huge creature was diving down, and towards the *Cormorant*. Once again, the line snapped tight. The small fishing boat swayed over to the side at a sharp angle, as the shark tugged the line deeper and deeper.

"We'll wait for it to tire itself out, lad," yelled Oliver. "Then we'll haul it in with the winch."

Sam knew to keep well away from the line, which was whipping its way across the edge of the boat as the creature on the end pulled one way then the other. For an hour, the two called to each other.

"It's going east!"

"It's diving underneath us!"

"It's heading out west again."

Then, the line stopped moving around the boat. It pointed straight towards the sun. Slowly, a small wave started to form around the front of the *Cormorant*. Sam was the first to see it and knew immediately what it meant.

"Grandad," he shouted. "It's pulling us along!"

The huge shark was so powerful, it was dragging the *Cormorant* further and further out to sea. Oliver started the engine, quickly pushing the gears into reverse. The water around the propeller thrashed white while the engine fought to keep the boat still. But it was no use as the shark, gradually picking up speed, towed the boat eastwards.

By midday, the *Cormorant* had lost sight of the land far behind. The sea had changed colour from blue to a deep, greeny-grey. Meanwhile, the shark kept surging forward, dragging the helpless *Cormorant* behind it.

Hours passed. The sun moved directly overhead and still the *Cormorant* and the shark, tied together, continued their journey. When the *Cormorant* pulled one way, the shark pulled the other. Slowly, the sun began heading towards the opposite horizon. As more hours passed and the light began to fade, Oliver tried everything. He tried to swing his boat around, and head in the other direction. The engine groaned and spluttered at full power, but still the *Cormorant* kept heading further out to sea.

Night fell as Oliver and Sam tried slowly winching in the line. But the bolts holding the winch on deck creaked and groaned, and the boat tilted over so much that they had to stop.

By midnight, Oliver and Sam knew they were in trouble — deep trouble. No matter how hard they tried, they realised they could not win the battle.

The shark seemed to realise the same thing. It gradually turned, and started to circle the *Cormorant*. As the night drew on, both boat and shark slowly moved around each other, like two boxers trying to land a punch.

At last, just when it seemed the night would never end, the first of the sun's rays dawned over the horizon. The second day of the great tug-of-war had begun.

"There's only one thing left to try," said Oliver finally, in a tired voice. "It's risky — but at this rate, by the end of the week, we'll end up in South America."

He crunched the engine's gears, and increased the motor power to full speed. But, instead of tugging away from the line, the *Cormorant* surged forward — in the same direction as the shark.

Oliver urged the engine faster and faster.
Gradually, the *Cormorant* edged closer to the shark.
The line grew slack in the water, as the *Cormorant*
began to pick up speed.

Minutes later, Sam gave a cry.

"I see it!" he yelled excitedly. "It's incredible.
It looks like a torpedo!"

"Aye, lad," yelled Oliver, who had also spotted the speeding shape of the shark. The *Cormorant* was rattling and shaking as it gained on the shadow a few metres in front of it.

"Now, hold on," Oliver called urgently. Sam grabbed the railing, and held on for his life.

Oliver swung the *Cormorant* around instantly, until it was facing back towards the other horizon. He knew he had only a few seconds before the line grew tight again. The engine was working at full steam, and powered the *Cormorant* at top speed — in the *opposite* direction to the shark.

Seconds passed. Both the shark and the *Cormorant* sped in opposite directions. In an instant, as the line between them tightened, both stopped dead in the water.

The force of the line almost heaved the *Cormorant* out of the sea. Its bow lifted until the fishing vessel hung at a crazy angle half in the air. Every nut and bolt and rivet and nail in the boat creaked. The curved timber of the boat's hull seemed to swell with the strain. Oliver and Sam hung on for their lives as a huge wave washed over the back of the boat.

And, for a moment, nothing happened. The boat stood still, its engine screaming and straining.

With a sickening jolt and a noise like a train crashing, the *Cormorant* lurched forward and its bow smashed into the sea again. Sam cried out in amazement, as a huge white splash frothed the sea. Then he gasped in astonishment at the torn timber on the deck — where the winch had once been bolted. It was gone. And so was the shark.

Chapter 5

The One That Got Away

It took the whole day for the *Cormorant* to limp back to Fairtide Pier. As the evening light began to fade, the chug-chug of the boat's engine floated across the water. A crowd of anxious people were gathered on the wharf. Oliver and Sam were surprised to see a line of lights and lanterns swaying along the length of the pier. A great cheer arose from their waiting friends as the *Cormorant* finally arrived home.

"Ahoy there," Oliver called out. "What's going on?"

"What indeed?" called out one of the other fishermen, while catching the rope that Sam threw to him. Tying it to the pier he replied, "You've been missing for two days! We all thought that the shark had *got* you."

Oliver laughed, pushed his captain's cap backwards and scratched his head.

"You should all know me better than that,"
he grinned. "You should have known that it was
me who would *get* the shark!"

There was much noise and fuss as the two
clambered off the *Cormorant* and on to the pier.
Everyone wanted to know exactly what had
happened, but Oliver and Sam suddenly felt too
exhausted to talk. Then, the crowd that had
gathered started to look embarrassed.

"Now what's the matter?" asked Oliver. One of the fishermen started to laugh.

"Well, we thought you'd been eaten," he said. "So we started a collection to buy you a memorial."

Oliver raised his bushy eyebrows. The fisherman drew a thick wad of notes from his pocket. "What'll we do with all this money now?" he asked.

Oliver grinned, and looked around at all the people on the pier. He nodded back towards the gaping hole where the winch had once been bolted on to the *Cormorant's* deck.

"If it's OK with you, I've got just the thing to spend it on," he said, smiling. "I'm sorry we spoiled your plans for a memorial. But how about a memorial winch?"

Somehow it seemed like a fitting way to spend the money. Within a week, a shiny new winch was fitted to the deck of the *Cormorant*. Attached to its side was a tiny brass plaque proclaiming 'Fairtide Memorial Winch: In Memory of the One That Got Away'.

"Fairtide Memorial Winch: In Memory of the One That Got Away."